This is a Borzoi Book
published by Alfred A. Knopf, Inc.

 Published in the United
States of America by Alfred A. Knopf,
Inc., New York. Distributed by Random
House, Inc., New York. Originally
published in Great Britain in 1993 by
Julia MacRae Books, a division of
Random House UK Ltd.

ISBN 0-679-84737-5 (trade)
Library of Congress Number: 93-20210

First American Edition
Manufactured in Hong Kong
1 3 5 7 9 10 8 6 4 2

The Big Baby

A Little Joke

ANTHONY BROWNE

ALFRED A. KNOPF : NEW YORK

Everyone said that John Young's dad
was young for his age.

He did have young clothes

and young hair styles.

He liked very loud rock music,

and he had a whole den full of toys.

Mr. Young liked being young,
and so he tried to stay that way.
Every morning he cycled.
(Well, *nearly* every morning . . .
well . . . sometimes.)

It was called ELIXA DE YOOF, and that night he eagerly drank the whole bottle.

Well, John's very fond of his dad, really,
but when his mum called him into their bedroom
the next morning, John just burst out laughing.
There in bed with his mother was a baby –
with his dad's face!

"He's *really* done it now, hasn't he?"
said Mrs. Young, and there was just a
little bit of a smile on her face too.

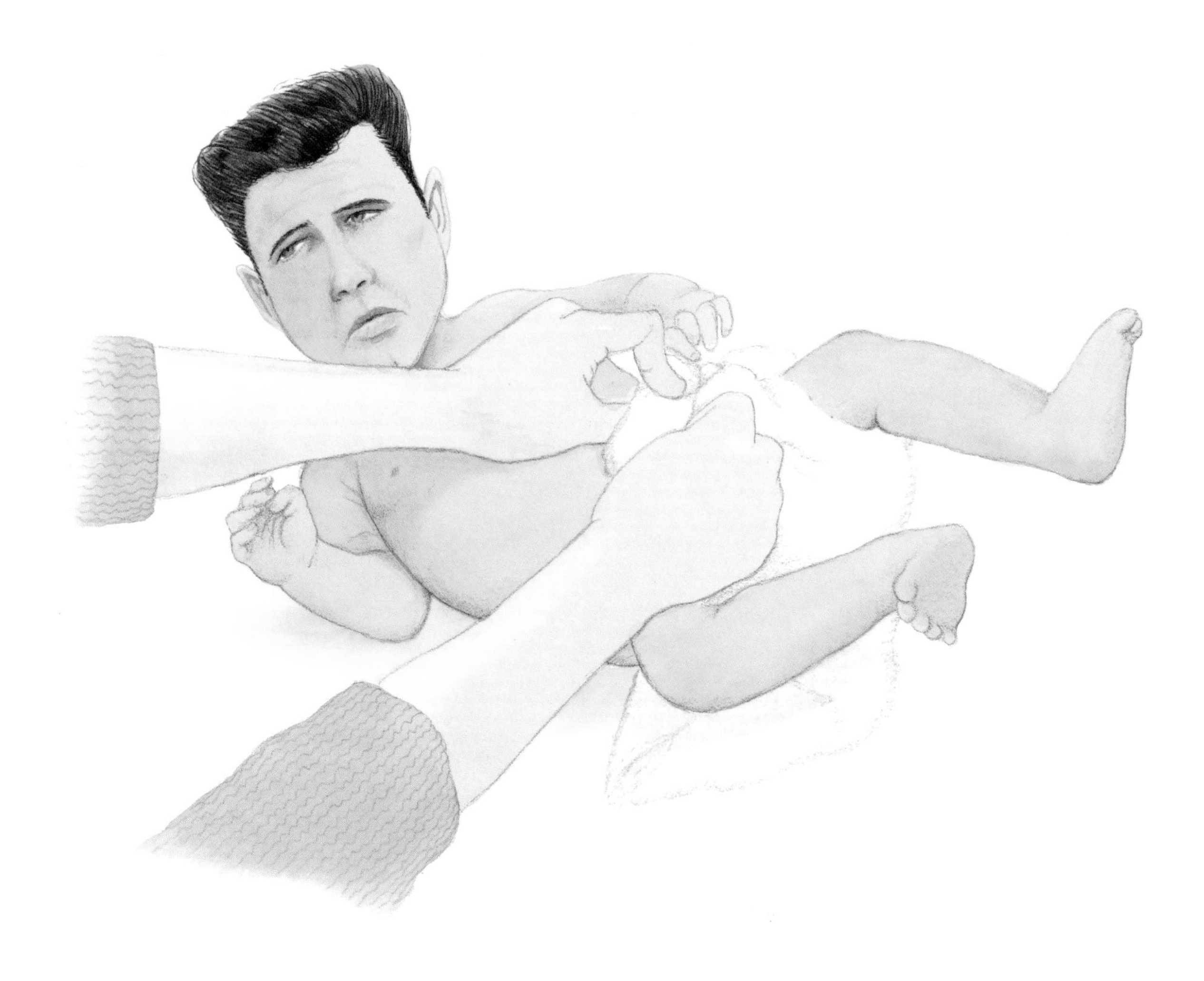

“The first thing we must do is put a diaper on him, he’s soaking wet,” she said. “John, can you get one from the bottom drawer while I clean him up?” Mr. Young tried to say something, but all he came out with was, “Ga-ga-ga-gaaa.”

Afterward Mrs. Young carried him downstairs for breakfast, and John fetched his old high-chair from the basement. His dad made a real mess of his muesli.

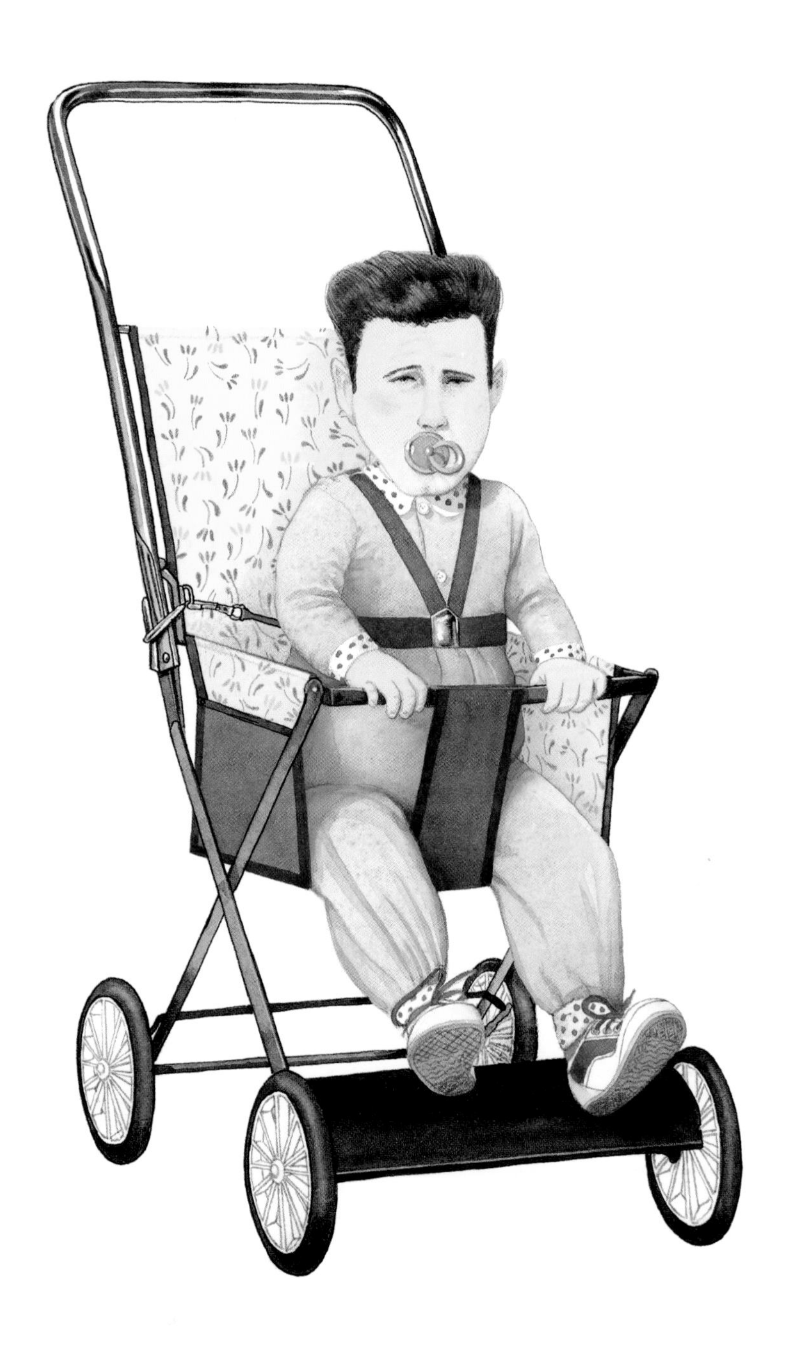

They took him for a walk later, and everyone
stopped and made a big fuss over him.

He didn't seem to enjoy that much. John's mum had to say that he was a friend's baby and she was looking after him. Mr. Young tried to say something, but all they could hear was "Boggaboggabogga."

When they got back home, Mrs. Young changed his diaper.

John tried playing with him and very carefully built him a tower, but as usual Mr. Young didn't seem interested in playing with his son.

He cried and cried, so Mrs. Young sat him on the potty. But it didn't help. Poor Mr. Young looked so silly that John felt quite sorry for him.

John's mum put his dad to bed
and he slept for hours.

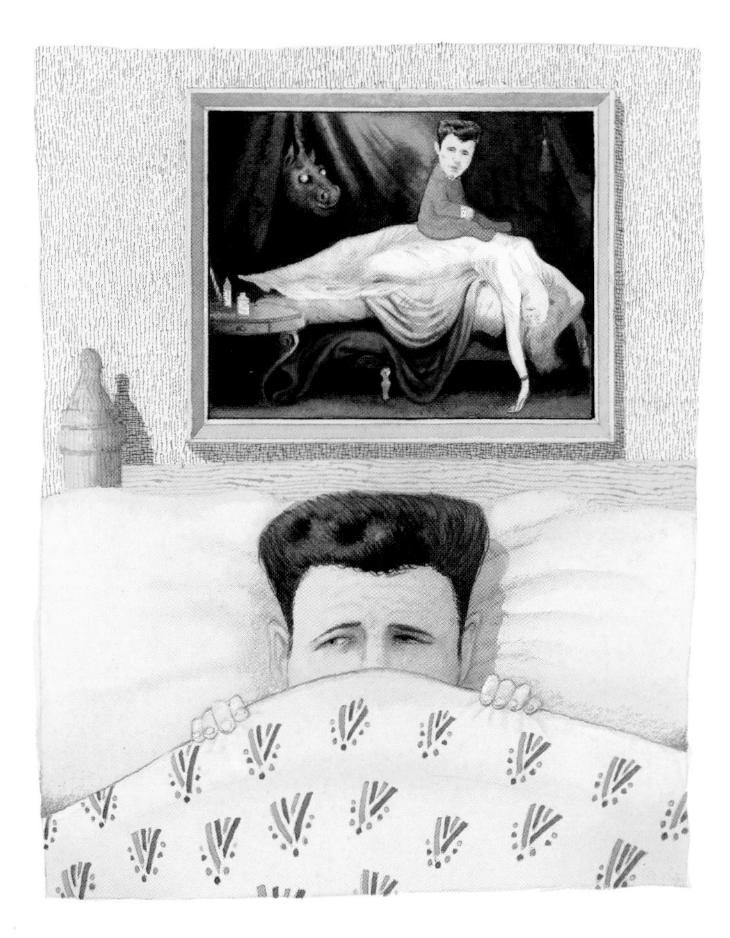

Much later they heard Mr. Young's "poorly" voice,
"C-can you come upstairs?"
They dashed up into his room.
There was John's dad, back to normal.
"I've had a TERRIBLE dream," he wailed.
"Oh, poor baby," said Mrs. Young.
"But how did *you* know?" asked Mr. Young.
She looked at John and smiled.
"Hey, Dad!" said John. "Go and look in the mirror."

And he saw his first gray hair.